TIME HAS STOPPED

TIME HAS STOPPED

KENNETH HAINES

Kenneth Haines
Time Has Stopped

Published by Spines Publishing Platform
ISBN: 979-8-89691-339-9

CONTENTS

1

THE DESERT MIRAGE

The morning sun rose, casting long shadows across the golden desert sands. In the distance, a caravan of camels ambled slowly across the parched earth, their riders slumped in the saddles, weary and beaten by the relentless heat.

The shimmering mirage of the rising sun made the landscape appear dreamlike, the vast expanse of the desert stretching endlessly before them. Each step taken by the camels stirred up small clouds of dust, blending with the heat waves that danced on the horizon.

The riders, cloaked in tattered robes, were silent, their eyes scanning the horizon for any sign of respite. The journey had been long, and the harsh desert had taken its toll. Yet, they pressed on, driven by a flicker of hope that somewhere beyond the sands, there lay a sanctuary.

Amidst the sea of dunes, the caravan moved forward, a testament to human endurance and the relentless pursuit of survival. The desert, with its unforgiving beauty, held secrets yet to be discovered and challenges yet to be faced.

As the caravan trudged through the endless dunes, they encountered relics that seemed out of place in the desert's expanse. Old wooden hulls of ships, their skeletons half-buried in sand, stood as haunting reminders of a time long gone. The weathered timbers and rusting iron whispered stories of an ancient ocean, a world where water once dominated these lands.

Seeing these remnants, the riders understood the full magnitude of the desert's transformation. What was once a thriving marine ecosystem had turned into a barren wasteland, where water was now a scarce and highly valuable resource. Each hull they passed told a tale of the earth's ever-changing face, a testament to nature's relentless progression.

Elara, the leader of the caravan, paused to touch one of the shipwrecks, her fingers tracing the weathered wood. "This was once a sea," she murmured, the realization both humbling and sobering. "Now, it's a desert, and water is the most precious treasure."

The group continued their journey with a newfound sense of awe and urgency. They were not just seeking survival—they were part of a grand cycle of change, adapting to a world reshaped by time and nature.

The sun climbed higher, its relentless heat beating down on the caravan. The temperature soared, and the once-bearable morning gave way to the harsh, midday desert.

The camels, sturdy yet tired, began to slow, their need for rest evident. The travelers, equally weary, felt the fatigue setting in, each step becoming a struggle against the blistering sand and oppressive heat.

Elara raised a hand, signaling for the group to halt. "We need to rest. The camels can't go on, and neither can we," she said, her voice steady but strained.

They found a small, shaded area beneath a rocky outcrop, the only respite in the vast desert expanse. The camels were relieved of their burdens, allowed to lie down and drink what little water they had left.

The travelers sat in the shade, grateful for the momentary relief. They shared sips of water, careful to conserve their precious supply. Each drop was a lifeline in the unforgiving desert.

Arin looked out at the shimmering horizon, his eyes squinting against the glare. "We need to find water soon," he said, voicing the concern they all felt.

Elara nodded. "We will. Rest now. We need our strength for the journey ahead."

With that, the group settled in, finding solace in the brief respite. The desert stretched on, but for now, they had each other and the strength to keep moving forward. The heat grew unbearable as they continued their journey. Suddenly, one of the camels lifted its head and started trotting faster, sensing something the riders couldn't yet see. The other camels followed suit, their instincts driving them forward. The riders clung to their saddles, puzzled by their camels' sudden urgency.

As they crested a high red dirt mound, the sight before them brought a glimmer of hope. There, amidst the endless expanse of sand, stood a lone palm tree, its green fronds swaying gently in the hot breeze.

Elara's heart leapt. "An oasis!" she cried out, her voice filled with a mix of relief and disbelief.

The sight of the palm tree spurred the group on, their fatigue momentarily forgotten. The promise of water and shade beckoned them, a sanctuary in the harsh desert.

The camels, driven by their instincts, quickened their pace, eager to reach the life-giving oasis. The weary travelers held on, driven by hope and the possibility of respite from the relentless heat.

As they approached the oasis, the sound of bubbling water reached their ears, and the sight of a crystal-clear spring confirmed their hopes. The group dismounted, rushing to the water's edge. They drank deeply, their spirits lifted by the refreshing coolness.

In this moment of relief, the travelers found renewed strength. The desert had tested them, but their determination had led them to this haven. With water to quench their thirst and shade to protect them from the sun, they were ready to face whatever challenges lay ahead.

Their moment of relief was short-lived. As they drank, the palm tree and water slowly began to vanish, the cool liquid turning to sand in their hands. What they had thought was an oasis was merely a mirage, a cruel trick of the desert.

The group, disheartened and thirsty once more, gathered their strength. Elara, though shaken, remained resolute. "We can't let this break us. We must keep moving," she urged.

Jax nodded, his determination renewed. "The desert may try to deceive us, but we'll find the real oasis. We have to."

With heavy hearts but steadfast resolve, they remounted their camels and continued their journey. The desert was relentless, but so were they. Together, they would persevere, driven by the hope that somewhere beyond the mirages, a true sanctuary awaited them.

As the sun dipped below the horizon, the sky transformed into a palette of deep oranges and purples. The dry wind picked up, sweeping across the red sands and erasing any traces of their journey. The desert seemed to conspire to hide their presence, the shifting sands a reminder of the world's constant state of flux.

The travelers felt the chill of the evening set in, a stark contrast to the day's blistering heat. They gathered closer, sharing what little warmth they could, the camels huddling beside them.

Elara looked out at the fading light, her mind racing with thoughts of what lay ahead. "We need to find shelter soon," she said, her voice steady but urgent.

Jax nodded, his eyes scanning the darkening landscape. "Let's keep moving, but stay close. We can't afford to get separated."

The group moved forward, guided by the faint light of the stars and the cool breeze that whispered through the desert night. They walked in silence, each step taken with the hope of finding a safe haven.

The desert, with all its challenges, had not broken their spirit.

Together, they would continue their journey, driven by the belief that somewhere beyond the shifting sands, a new beginning awaited them. During the night they couldn't see much of what was outside so once they settled in one of the empty adobe homes and set up the camels in another they settled down to rest.

2

THE HIDDEN OASIS

As dawn broke, casting a soft glow over the adobe homes, Arin stirred from his sleep. The quiet of the morning was a stark contrast to the challenges they had faced the day before. Carefully, he peered outside, his eyes catching sight of an old, weathered well just beyond the ridge.

Curiosity piqued, Arin slipped out quietly, not wanting to wake the others. The cold morning air bit at his skin, but the promise of the well drew him forward. As he approached, he could see the structure was ancient, its stones worn smooth by time and weather.

He leaned over cautiously, peering into the dark depths. A faint, hopeful glimmer of moisture caught his eye. His heart quickened—could this be the source of water they so desperately needed?

Arin hurried back to the adobe home, gently rousing Elara and the others. "Wake up, everyone. I think I found something!"

The group quickly gathered their belongings and followed Arin to the well. With a sense of anticipation, they began to draw up the bucket, praying that it wasn't another cruel mirage.

As the bucket emerged, they saw it—clear, fresh water. The group erupted in cheers, their spirits lifted by the discovery. They took turns drinking deeply, the cool water a balm for their weary bodies and souls.

Elara smiled, tears of relief in her eyes. "This water... it's a gift. We can rest here, gather our strength, and plan our next steps."

The adobe homes, once just a place of refuge for the night, had become a sanctuary. The discovery of the well was a beacon of hope, guiding them forward in their journey through the desert.

Jax methodically explored the empty adobe homes, his eyes scanning for anything useful. Among the abandoned structures, he found broken wooden furniture—chairs, stools, and even a table scattered in pieces.

"Perfect," he muttered to himself, gathering the wood. This would be more than enough to start a small fire and keep them warm during the cold desert nights.

Back at their makeshift camp, Jax piled the wood together. Elara, Arin helped arrange the pieces to ensure the fire would burn efficiently. With a few strikes of flint, the fire crackled to life, its warm glow illuminating their faces and providing a much-needed comfort against the desert chill. They sat around the fire, feeling a sense of accomplishment and relief. The discovery of the adobe homes, the well, and now the wood for a fire, had turned their dire situation into a more hopeful one.

Arin looked at the flames, a thoughtful expression on his face. "It's amazing how even the smallest finds can make such a big difference."

Elara nodded, her eyes reflecting the dancing firelight. "We've come a long way. We can rest here and gather our strength for whatever lies ahead." Liora and Maia, the youngest of the group, huddled together near the fire. Though they were just children, their resilience was evident. They stayed close, not wanting to get in the way of the adults but finding comfort in each other's presence.

Elara noticed their quiet forms and moved closer, wrapping a blanket around them. "You two are stronger than you know," she said softly, her voice filled with warmth and encouragement.

Jax, tending to the fire, glanced over with a reassuring smile. "We're all in this together. You're an important part of our group."

The fire's warmth enveloped them all, providing not just physical heat but a sense of unity and security. Despite the challenges of the desert, they had found moments of peace and togetherness, forging bonds that would carry them through whatever lay ahead.

3

THE RELENTLESS JOURNEY

After several nights of rest, the group felt their strength returning. The adobe homes had provided much-needed shelter, and the well had quenched their thirst. With renewed resolve, they packed their belongings, ready to face the harsh desert and the relentless sun once again.

Elara led the way, her eyes scanning the horizon for any signs of hope. Jax walked beside her, his hand resting on Jake's head for reassurance. Arin, Liora, and Maia followed closely, their spirits lifted by the temporary respite they had enjoyed.

The desert stretched out before them, an endless sea of red sands and shimmering heat waves. Each step they took was a testament to their resilience and determination. The sun beat down mercilessly, but they pressed on, driven by the hope that somewhere beyond the dunes, a new beginning awaited them.

As they journeyed through the shifting sands, they remained vigilant, their bond growing stronger with each passing moment. They knew the desert would continue to test them, but together, they were ready to face whatever challenges lay ahead.

As they continued their trek through the harsh desert, the heat was becoming unbearable. Suddenly, they heard an unfamiliar sound—clanging metal echoing in the distance. Jax and Arin quickly huddled the group together, sharing wary glances.

Curiosity and caution mingled in their eyes as they decided to investigate the source of the noise.

With Jake leading the way, they walked several miles, the clanging growing louder. The sun cast long shadows as it dipped closer to the horizon. Finally, they crested a dune and their eyes widened in astonishment.

Before them was an enormous, ancient statue partially buried in the sand. A colossal stone hand protruded from the ground, grasping a torch that seemed to defy the ages. The hand's fingers were curled around the base of the torch, its immense size dwarfing the travelers. The torch itself, though unlit, was intricately detailed, suggesting it once held great significance.

Elara stepped forward, her breath catching. "This... this is incredible. Who could have built such a thing?"

Jax examined the stonework, running his fingers over the weathered surface. "Whoever they were, they had skills beyond anything we've seen."

The group stood in awe, the statue's sheer size and craftsmanship a stark contrast to the desolate landscape around them. The mystery of the giant hand and its torch added a new layer of intrigue to their journey, hinting at ancient civilizations and untold stories buried beneath the desert sands.

As they pondered the significance of their discovery, the desert winds began to pick up, swirling around the statue and the travelers. The clanging sound, now understood to be the shifting of ancient metal against stone, continued to resonate in their minds.

With renewed curiosity and determination, they knew their journey had taken another unexpected turn, leading them deeper into the mysteries of the desert.

Liora's eyes widened with recognition as she stared at the colossal hand. "I've heard stories about this statue," she said, her voice trembling with excitement. "It once stood at the wharf of a great city in the ocean."

Elara, listening to Liora's words, suddenly sank to her knees. Memories of tales told in her childhood came flooding back. "The

Hand of Freedom," she whispered, eyes filling with wonder. "If those stories are true, then this desert was once a vast sea."

The group gathered closer, the weight of the revelation sinking in. The hand, now a relic of a bygone era, stood as a testament to the transformation of the world. The realization that they were standing in what was once an ocean, now reduced to an arid desert, filled them with awe and a renewed sense of purpose.

Jax placed a reassuring hand on Elara's shoulder. "We've uncovered something incredible," he said. "Let's use this knowledge to guide us forward. If the Hand of Freedom still stands, perhaps there are other remnants of the past that can help us find a way through this desert."

With renewed determination, the group set their sights on the journey ahead. The desert had revealed a piece of its ancient history, and they were ready to continue their quest, guided by the stories and the hope that lay within the sands.

They trekked on hoping to find shelter but all they could see was red sand. In the distance A massive wind storm was brewing and it was heading for them. They had to make hast back to the hand with the torch to get behind it.

charged with tension as they swiftly tie ropes around the hand, securing the camels in a makeshift pen. The wind grows louder and more violent as they dig into the red sand, pressing their bodies against the hand in a desperate bid to shield themselves from the storm's fury.

The storm hits with a deafening roar, and for a moment, it feels as though the world is collapsing around them. But they hold fast, clinging to the hand and each other, braving the chaos together. The sand whips around them, but they know they've made the best decision they could in such dire circumstances. They just have to wait it out and hope the storm passes soon. The sound of the raging wind seems endless, and every moment feels like an eternity.

The ropes didn't hold and the camels scattered leaving them without something to ride for passage and luckily they didn't loose any supplies but being stuck here against a hand and torch, The situation just turned even more dire. The loss of their camels leaves them without a means of transportation, and the vast, red desert suddenly seems even more daunting. Huddled against the hand with the torch, they take stock of their supplies, feeling a mix of relief and anxiety. The storm has passed, but the silence that follows feels eerie and unsettling.

The scorching sun begins to rise, casting long shadows and intensifying the heat. They know they need to find another way to continue their journey, but without the camels, their options are limited.

Determined to survive, they start brainstorming. Perhaps they could build a signal fire to attract attention, or maybe they could create makeshift sleds from the supplies to drag them across the sand. The hand with the torch, once a mere shelter, now stands as a beacon of hope in their minds, reminding them that they must press on and not give up.

4
THE DISCOVERY

On the other side of this enormous hand the sand built up against it and Jax was able to get up to the torch and saw an opening inside it, he called down to the others to gather their supplies and follow him. As they scramble to gather their supplies, the atmosphere buzzes with a renewed sense of purpose. Climbing up the sand dunes, they reach the opening and peek inside.

The interior is dimly lit, and the torch's light flickers gently against the ancient stone walls. The space looks like it hasn't been disturbed in ages. They cautiously step inside, their footsteps echoing softly. Inside, they find a narrow passage leading deeper into the structure. They share determined glances, knowing this might be their only chance to find safety and perhaps even clues to survive the desert.

There was a ladder against the wall or inside the arm leading downward, Jax and the other male of the group started to climb down while the others huddled in the torch. The tension builds as Jax and the other man carefully descend the ladder, their footsteps echoing softly in the hollow arm of the structure. Each rung they touch feels cool and ancient, as if they're journeying into a forgotten part of history. The others huddle together in the torch's chamber, their hearts racing with a mix of fear and hope.

As Jax and his companion reach the bottom, they find themselves in a dimly lit chamber. The walls are adorned with ancient carvings and symbols, hinting at a long-lost civilization. The air is cool and slightly musty, a stark contrast to the scorching desert outside. They take a moment to let their eyes adjust to the darkness before proceeding further.

Exploring the chamber, they find what appears to be a passageway leading deeper into the structure. They call up to the others, signaling them to come down and join in the exploration. With renewed determination, the group prepares to uncover the secrets hidden within this mysterious place.

The group, filled with anticipation, climbs the spiraling staircase, each step echoing in the hollow structure. As they reach the top, they find themselves on a platform which was once used as a viewing, now covered totally buried underneath the red sand.

Mia, intrigued by an old picture on the wall, carefully wipes away the dust and grime. As the image becomes clear, it depicts a vibrant city by the water, bustling with life. She excitedly points out the landmarks, realizing that this place once served as an observation point for people to gaze out over the water and the massive city below.

The group's discovery brings a mix of emotions—wonder at the ancient civilization that once thrived here, and hope that they might find more clues or resources to help them on their journey. This newfound perspective also raises questions about the fate of the city and what mysteries lie hidden beneath the sands.

With renewed determination, they decide to explore further, hoping to uncover more secrets and perhaps find a way to survive and continue their quest. The journey continues, filled with the promise of discovery and adventure. What will they find next?

Finding an ancient, winding path that seems to have withstood the test of time. The group finds this staircase spiraling downwards, leading them towards ground level. As they carefully navigate each step, the dim light from their torches flickers against the walls, revealing more carvings and symbols from the lost civilization.

As they descend, the atmosphere grows cooler, and the air becomes more humid, hinting that they might be getting closer to an underground water source or perhaps another hidden chamber. The staircase could open up into a vast underground cavern, offering new opportunities and challenges for the group.

As they reach ground level, the group's torchlight reveals an astounding sight. The walls surrounding them are adorned with forgotten pictures and artifacts, remnants of a long-lost civilization. The intricate carvings and faded images tell stories of a once-thriving city, filled with people and culture. The group pauses, marveling at the history preserved within these ancient walls.

The ground beneath them opens up into large, spacious areas, and they notice the remnants of an old rail system. The tracks, though covered in dust and debris, hint at a sophisticated transportation network that once connected different parts of the city. The rail system extends into the darkness, offering a potential path for the group to follow.

With renewed hope, they realize that this rail system might lead them to more clues about the ancient city or even an exit from the structure. Carefully, they begin to explore the area, examining the artifacts and studying the rail tracks. The sense of discovery and adventure pulses through them, driving them forward into the unknown.

The group, exhausted from their journey and the discovery, settles down amidst the ancient artifacts and carvings. They gather whatever useful items they can find, their torches casting flickering shadows on the walls. Jax, resourceful as always, sifts through the debris and manages to start a small fire. The warm glow of the fire provides both comfort and light, lifting their spirits.

As they rest around the fire, the group takes a moment to reflect on their journey so far. The firelight dances on their faces, revealing a mix of determination and exhaustion. They share stories and thoughts, drawing strength from each other's presence. The ancient chamber, once a silent witness to a bygone era, now becomes a temporary sanctuary for these modern-day explorers.

With the fire crackling softly, they drift into a much-needed sleep, their dreams filled with visions of the ancient city and the mysteries yet to be uncovered. As the night wears on, the chamber remains a silent guardian, holding secrets that await their discovery.

During there time of slumber something big an fear some was headed towards them, something they never seen out on the red sands. Something that will disrupt this group and wishing they never came down here.

5

TRAVEL THE BLACKENED RAIL

The group decided to remain in the safety of the statue's base for a few days, using the time to recover and strategize. Their days were filled with the careful exploration of the ancient pictures and artifacts that adorned the walls. Among the dusty relics, they discovered old maps scattered across the floor. These maps held the key to understanding the rail system they had stumbled upon.

As they examined the maps, they pieced together a clearer picture of what the rails were used for. The rails once connected various parts of the vast city, providing an efficient means of transportation for its inhabitants. The maps also included directions and landmarks, guiding them through the labyrinthine network of tracks.

Armed with this new knowledge, the group felt a renewed sense of purpose. They knew they had to venture onto the rail system, hoping it would lead them to safety or perhaps even the answers to the mysteries of the ancient civilization.

With determination, they gathered their supplies and prepared to travel the blackened rail. The journey ahead was uncertain and fraught with danger, but they knew they had to move forward. The memory of Arin's sacrifice fueled their resolve, pushing them to continue despite the fear and uncertainty.

As they set foot on the ancient tracks, the weight of the unknown pressed upon them. The rail system stretched into the darkness, offering both a path and a promise. The group moved cautiously, their steps echoing in the silence, ready to face whatever lay ahead on this perilous journey.

The journey along the blackened rail was treacherous, with debris littering the tracks and sections twisted and ripped from the ground. Jax and Elara kept the younger ones safely between them, taking great care to move silently and avoid making any loud noises that might attract unwanted attention.

Time seemed to stretch on interminably, the oppressive darkness and silence making every moment feel like an eternity. After what felt like days but was only a matter of hours, they stumbled upon an old, rusted rail car lying on its side. The sight of the dilapidated rail car brought both a sense of unease and curiosity.

Cautiously, they approached the wreck, peering inside through broken windows and gaps in the metal. The interior was a haunting reminder of the past, with seats now torn and rotting away. The once bustling rail car, filled with passengers and life, was now a ghostly relic of a bygone era.

Despite the eerie atmosphere, the group decided to explore the rail car, hoping to find any useful items or clues that might aid them in their journey. They moved carefully, their torches casting long shadows on the decayed seats and crumbling walls. The rail car held an air of mystery, and they couldn't help but wonder what stories it had witnessed before being abandoned to the sands of time.

With the soft glow of their torchlight illuminating the dark underground realm, the group cautiously moved forward, ever mindful of the lurking dangers. The ancient walls around them told a silent story, marked by signs that had once guided the inhabitants of this lost civilization.

Some of the signs were still legible, offering cryptic messages that hinted at the purpose and layout of the rail system. Others were too faded by the passage of time to decipher, leaving gaps in their understanding. The most intriguing of all were the red pointers and arrows painted on the walls, directing them towards an unknown destination.

These arrows, though weathered, seemed more recent than the other signs, suggesting that someone else had once navigated these corridors. The group followed the arrows with a mix of curiosity and caution, their footsteps echoing softly in the darkness.

As they ventured deeper, the air grew cooler and more humid, hinting at the presence of underground water sources or perhaps another hidden chamber. The red arrows guided their way, and with each step, they felt both hope and trepidation.

The group, weary from their journey, reached a raised platform. Jax and Elara worked together to lift the others onto it, ensuring everyone was safely above ground level. Once everyone was on the platform, Jax urged them to stay close to the wall for safety while he cautiously scouted the surrounding area.

The darkness pressed in around him as he moved silently, his senses on high alert for any signs of danger. He gathered debris and other useful materials along the way, determined to create a small fire to provide warmth and comfort for the night.

Returning to the group, Jax used the debris to kindle a small fire, the flickering flames casting a soft glow on their tired faces. The warmth and light brought a sense of relief, allowing them to rest and regain their strength. The platform, though an unfamiliar refuge, offered a temporary sanctuary from the dangers of the underground realm.

As they settled down around the fire, the group shared quiet conversations and whispered hopes for the journey ahead. The fire crackled softly, a beacon of resilience in the face of uncertainty. They knew that the road ahead would be challenging, but together, they were determined to overcome whatever obstacles lay in their path.

Jax felt a gentle breeze brush against his face, accompanied by a faint, almost melodic sound from the far end of the platform. It was an unusual sensation, given the stillness of the underground realm. Curious and cautious, he whispered to Elara that he was going to investigate. Lighting his torch from the fire, he ventured into the darkness, the flickering flame casting shadows on the ancient walls.

Elara watched him go, concern etched on her face. She lay down beside the other two, ensuring they remained undisturbed in their slumber. Her ears were finely tuned to any sound, ready to spring into action at the slightest hint of danger.

Jax moved quietly, the soft glow of the torch revealing more of the forgotten past with each step. The sound grew slightly louder as he approached the far end of the platform. It was a strange, almost ethereal hum, unlike anything he had heard before. The air seemed to grow cooler, and the breeze brushed against his face once more, urging him onward.

Jax stood before the stairs, their ascent rendered impossible by the constant flow of water cascading down them. The sight was both intriguing and frustrating, as it hinted at something beyond but remained just out of reach. Bending down, he carefully smelled the water and then tasted it. The metallic scent was unmistakable, and the taste of iron confirmed his suspicion.

This discovery added another layer to the mystery of the ancient underground realm. The water, with its metallic properties, might have come from deep within the earth, perhaps from a hidden source or a long-forgotten reservoir. The presence of the stairs suggested there was something important above, but for now, it remained inaccessible.

Jax's mind raced with possibilities. Could there be another way to reach the upper levels? Or perhaps there was a means to stop the water flow? He knew he had to share this information with the group and discuss their next steps.

Returning to the platform, Jax relayed his findings to Elara and the others. The group gathered around, listening intently. The discovery of the stairs and the water added a new challenge to their journey, but it also fueled their determination to uncover the secrets of this ancient place.

Jax's resourcefulness shines through as he retrieves a small pan from their supplies. Carefully, he returns to the water source and fills the pan with the iron-scented water. Bringing it back to the platform, he places it over the small fire he had kindled earlier, watching as the water begins to heat up.

The group huddles close, the flickering flames providing a comforting warmth. As the water heats, the metallic scent fills the air, a reminder of the depths from which it came. Once the water reaches a boil, Jax removes it from the fire, allowing it to cool. After some time, the water becomes drinkable, its once strong iron taste now significantly milder.

This small victory brings a sense of relief and hope to the group. They carefully share the heated water, replenishing their strength and hydrating themselves. The experience reinforces their determination to adapt and survive in this challenging environment.

With their spirits lifted, the group gathers around the fire, discussing their next steps. The waterlogged stairs still pose a significant obstacle, but they are more determined than ever to find a way forward.

The realization sinks in that their sanctuary, though safe for now, is not a permanent solution. The group knows that they can't stay here forever. They need to continue their journey along the forgotten rails, pressing on despite the uncertainties that lie ahead.

After taking some time to rest, gather their strength, and make the most of the resources they have, they prepare to move forward. The maps and signs they discovered provide some guidance, but they know that the path will still be treacherous.

Jax, Elara, and the others pack up their supplies and extinguish the fire. With a renewed sense of determination, they begin their descent back onto the ancient tracks. The darkness stretches out before them, but the flicker of their torches lights the way. The rail system, once a vital part of a bustling city, now serves as their guide through the underground realm.

6
IT RETURNS

Step by step, they navigate the twisted and debris-laden tracks, ever vigilant for signs of danger and hidden secrets. The journey is far from over, but they are ready to face whatever challenges come their way.

The echoing noise from that ominous first day reverberated through the underground realm, growing louder with each passing moment. A chill of fear gripped everyone as they recognized the approaching sound of the mutated creature. The group's hearts pounded in unison, knowing that this time, there was no place to climb to safety.

Jax, ever the leader, signaled for everyone to stay close together and move cautiously. The flickering torchlight danced on their anxious faces as they tried to think of a plan. The rails beneath them offered no refuge, and the dark corridors seemed to close in, amplifying their fear.

They huddled close, whispering hurried strategies. Elara suggested they use the torches to create a barrier of light, hoping it might deter the creature or at least buy them some time. The group quickly set about lighting additional torches, arranging them in a semicircle to ward off the impending danger.

The noise grew louder, and the ground seemed to tremble as the creature drew nearer. The group's resolve hardened; they knew they had to face this threat head-on. With their makeshift light barrier in place, they readied themselves for the confrontation.

Will their plan work? Can they outsmart the mutated creature and survive this encounter?The creature's massive form loomed into the light, its grotesque appearance sending shivers down the spines of everyone in the group. But what they saw next was beyond belief. Perched on the creature's back was Arin, their lost companion. The sight was a heart-wrenching mix of relief and horror.

Arin's eyes met theirs, and for a brief moment, there was a flicker of recognition and sadness. It was clear that he had endured unimaginable suffering, yet his presence ignited a spark of hope amidst the fear. The creature, sensing the group's reactions, let out a menacing growl, its eyes glowing with an unnatural light.

Jax's mind raced with conflicting emotions. He knew they had to rescue Arin, but the creature's formidable strength posed a significant threat. Elara, her eyes filled with determination, grabbed Jax's arm and whispered, "We have to save him."

The group quickly devised a plan, knowing they had to act fast. They decided to use their torches and makeshift weapons to create a distraction, hoping to divert the creature's attention long enough to rescue Arin. With steely resolve, they prepared to face the mutated beast.

The tension was palpable as they put their plan into action. The torches flared brightly, and the group moved with coordinated precision. They called out to Arin, their voices filled with a mix of urgency and hope.

The tense atmosphere shifted dramatically as Arin's voice cut through the chaos, urgently calling out to Jax to halt his attack. The group watched in astonishment as Arin gently patted the creature's head, murmuring soothing words into its ear. The once fearsome beast seemed to respond to Arin's calm presence, lowering itself to the ground to allow him to slide down.

Arin's safe descent from the creature's back left the group in awe, their earlier fear replaced with a mix of relief and curiosity. It was evident that Arin had somehow formed a bond with the mutated creature, turning a potential threat into a surprising ally.

Jax and Elara exchanged bewildered glances, their minds racing with questions. How had Arin managed to communicate with the creature? What had he experienced during his time with it? The group's emotions were a whirlwind of disbelief, hope, and a newfound sense of wonder.

As Arin rejoined the group, he quickly explained how he had managed to connect with the creature during his captivity. The creature, though initially aggressive, had shown signs of intelligence and empathy. Arin's calm and patient approach had allowed him to gain its trust, ultimately leading to this unexpected alliance.

The group's journey had taken yet another unexpected turn, and with the creature now on their side, their chances of survival seemed to improve. The bond between Arin and the creature hinted at the possibility of uncovering even more secrets about the ancient underground realm.

As they journeyed through the labyrinthine tunnels, the younger ones rode atop the creature, their fear slowly replaced by a cautious curiosity. The creature, now a surprising ally, moved steadily, its presence offering a strange comfort amidst the ancient ruins.

Arin walked alongside Jax and Elara, sharing the harrowing tale of his time in captivity. He described how the creature initially treated him like a toy, a curiosity to be played with. Despite the terror and uncertainty, Arin had sensed a glimmer of intelligence and empathy in the creature's eyes. Over time, he had used gentle words and calm gestures to gain its trust, turning a potential adversary into a companion.

Jax and Elara listened intently, their admiration for Arin growing with each word. His resilience and ability to connect with the creature had not only saved his life but had also given the group a unique advantage in their journey. They marveled at the bond that had formed between Arin and the creature, a testament to the power of patience and understanding.

The tunnels stretched on before them, their path illuminated by the soft glow of their torches. With each step, the group grew more determined, their spirits buoyed by the unexpected alliance and the knowledge that they were not alone in this ancient underground realm.

As the tunnel inclined upwards, the group felt a mix of anticipation and trepidation. Reaching the next platform provided a welcome respite, and they quickly gathered onto it, feeling the strain of their journey in their tired muscles. The creature, sensing their need for rest, settled down beside the platform, its presence a comforting constant amidst the uncertainty.

The platform offered a brief moment of relief, and the group took the opportunity to catch their breath and reassess their situation. The creature's loyalty to Arin and its willingness to stay nearby spoke volumes about the bond they had formed. It was a silent guardian, watching over them as they strategized their next move.

The upward path of the tunnel hinted at new possibilities, and the group knew that they needed to stay vigilant. The platform, though a temporary haven, served as a reminder that their journey was far from over. With the creature by their side, they felt a renewed sense of determination to face whatever lay ahead.

As they rested, they shared quiet conversations, their voices filled with a mix of hope and resolve. The fire's warmth and the creature's steady presence provided a sense of security, allowing them to momentarily forget the dangers that lurked in the darkness.

Jax's mind raced back to the previous platform where they had found stairs leading upwards. With hope rekindled, he grabbed a torch and set off to investigate if this one had a similar escape route. The flickering flame illuminated the path ahead as he moved cautiously, searching for any sign of an upward passage.

After a few moments of exploration, Jax's torchlight revealed a set of stairs. However, his heart sank as he saw that the stairs were completely choked with red sand, right down to the platform. The realization hit him hard – there was no exit that way.

Returning to the group, Jax shared the disappointing news. The blocked stairs meant they would need to find another way forward. Elara and the others listened intently, their determination unwavering despite the setback. The creature, still resting beside the platform, seemed to sense their resolve.

7
LEAVING THE DARKNESS

The group gathered their thoughts and discussed their next move. They knew that continuing along the rails was their best option, despite the uncertainty and potential dangers. The red arrows and the ancient maps would guide them, and with the creature's presence, they felt a renewed sense of purpose.

As they prepared to move on, they remained vigilant, ready to face whatever challenges lay ahead. The story of their journey continues, driven by their resilience and the unbreakable bond they share.

After hours of navigating the treacherous tunnels, the group found themselves surrounded by a chaotic scene of twisted metal beams, broken chunks of cement, and red sand scattered everywhere. The unsettling sounds of creaking metal and debris falling from above added to the tension, creating an atmosphere of imminent danger.

Jax, ever vigilant, instructed everyone to stay back and let him and Arin scout ahead. Their torches cast eerie shadows on the ruined landscape, highlighting the precarious nature of their surroundings. The group watched with bated breath as Jax and Arin carefully made their way through the debris, their steps deliberate and cautious.

The air was thick with anticipation as Jax and Arin moved

forward, their senses on high alert for any signs of further collapse or hidden threats. The twisted metal beams and shattered cement told a story of destruction and decay, a stark reminder of the challenges they faced in this underground realm.

As they ventured deeper into the chaotic landscape, Jax and Arin's bond grew stronger, their shared experiences forging a sense of trust and camaraderie. They knew that their careful exploration was crucial to ensuring the safety of the entire group.

As Arin and Jax continued their cautious exploration, they stumbled upon remnants of machinery and vehicles, unlike anything they had ever seen. Some were smashed and flattened, their original forms barely recognizable. Among the debris, Arin spotted something intriguing—a vehicle with seats both in the front and back. The sight piqued his curiosity, prompting him to crawl inside cautiously.

"Jax, look at this!" Arin called out, his voice echoing in the cavernous space. He had found a round object attached to the vehicle's interior. As he turned it, to his amazement, the flattened components of the vehicle moved back and forth, responding to his manipulation.

Jax approached, his eyes wide with wonder. The round object Arin was turning was unlike anything they had seen in their world. It seemed to have once controlled the vehicle's movements, hinting at a level of sophistication in the ancient civilization's technology.

Arin's discovery added a new layer of intrigue to their journey. The group's understanding of the underground realm and its history deepened with each new find. Despite the danger and uncertainty, their sense of wonder and curiosity kept them moving forward.

With the weight of their discoveries still fresh in their minds, Jax and Arin returned to the group and recounted their findings. They described the strange, flattened vehicles and the remnants of ancient technology, sparking a mix of curiosity and apprehension among the others.

Jax, ever mindful of the group's well-being, suggested they

take some time to rest before pressing forward. The journey had been exhausting, and a period of respite would allow them to gather their strength and mentally prepare for the challenges ahead.

The group settled down on the platform, their makeshift camp providing a temporary refuge from the surrounding chaos. The creature remained close by, its watchful presence offering a sense of security. As they rested, they shared quiet conversations, their thoughts wandering to the mysteries they had yet to uncover.

With their spirits bolstered by Arin's unexpected alliance with the creature and the intriguing discoveries they had made, the group felt a renewed sense of purpose. They knew that the path ahead would be fraught with danger, but together, they were determined to navigate the unknown and uncover the secrets of the ancient underground realm.

After a much-needed rest, the group felt a renewed sense of determination. The challenges they had faced so far had only strengthened their resolve. It was time to leave the darkness behind and forge a new path forward.

Jax, Elara, Arin, and the rest of the group gathered their supplies, their torches casting a warm glow on their determined faces. The creature, their unexpected ally, stood by, ready to continue the journey with them. The tunnel before them stretched into the unknown, but they were ready to face whatever lay ahead.

With a final glance at their makeshift camp, they set off along the blackened rails. The sense of anticipation hung heavy in the air as they moved forward, guided by the red arrows and the ancient maps. The darkness seemed to recede with each step, replaced by the growing light of their torches.

As they walked, they encountered new sights and sounds, remnants of a once-thriving civilization. Twisted metal, broken machinery, and faded signs told the story of a world lost to time. Yet, amidst the ruins, there was a sense of hope and possibility. The group's journey had become a quest for discovery, not just for survival.

The tunnel began to incline once more, and the air grew fresher, hinting at the promise of the surface. Their hearts quickened with excitement as they sensed they were nearing the end of the underground realm. The thought of leaving the darkness behind and stepping into the light filled them with renewed energy.

The group's hopes of stepping into the light were momentarily dashed as they emerged from the tunnel to find themselves surrounded by endless layers of red sand. The sight was disheartening, but their determination remained unshaken. The vast, desolate expanse before them was a stark reminder of the challenges they still faced.

8
TIME QUIT TICKING

The red sand stretched out as far as the eye could see, with no immediate shelter in sight. The harsh sun beat down on them, intensifying the heat and making the journey even more arduous. Yet, despite the daunting landscape, the group's resolve grew stronger.

Jax, Elara, Arin, and the others knew they had to press on, guided by the knowledge and experiences they had gained during their time in the underground realm. The creature, their loyal companion, moved steadily beside them, offering silent support as they navigated the unforgiving terrain.

As they trudged through the red sand, the group kept their spirits up by sharing stories and memories, reminding each other of their shared purpose and the bonds they had formed. The journey was far from over, but together, they felt capable of overcoming any obstacle.

The creature with them shakes off the younger ones and started running ahead till it was out of site, as it was running away it was dropping their supplies they also had on its back there was no sound to what made it act this way.

The group's hearts sank as they watched the creature, their once loyal companion, shake off the younger ones and bolt ahead.

As it ran, their precious supplies tumbled from its back, scattering across the red sand. The creature soon disappeared from sight, leaving the group in a state of shock and dismay.

Realizing the urgency of the situation, Jax, Elara, Arin, and the others quickly sprang into action. They rushed to gather the scattered supplies, knowing that every item was crucial to their survival. The harsh sun and endless sand made the task arduous, but their determination drove them to collect everything they could find.

With the supplies secured, they regrouped and assessed their situation. The loss of the creature, coupled with the uncertainty of their surroundings, made the journey even more daunting. Yet, they knew they had to keep moving forward.

Jax took a deep breath, trying to calm his racing thoughts. "We'll make it through this," he said, his voice steady despite the turmoil. "We just have to stick together and keep pushing forward."

The group nodded in agreement, their resolve strengthened by Jax's words. They set off once more, their steps heavy but their spirits unbroken. The vast red desert lay before them, a daunting challenge, but they faced it with courage and unity.

The gravity of their situation weighed heavily on them as they shared the last of their water. Each drop felt precious, a stark reminder of the limited resources they had left. The vast, unforgiving desert stretched out in every direction, and they knew that time was running out.

Despite the pressing urgency, the group remained united and determined. Jax, Elara, Arin, and the others exchanged looks of resolve, understanding that they needed to make every moment count. Their survival depended on their ability to work together and find a solution in the harsh environment.

"We need to keep moving," Jax said, his voice steady but firm. "There has to be something out there. A source of water, a shelter —anything."

Elara nodded, her eyes filled with a mix of hope and determination. "We can't give up now. We've come too far."

With that, they gathered their supplies and set off once more, their steps heavy but purposeful. The red sand seemed to go on forever, but they kept their eyes on the horizon, searching for any sign of hope. The sun beat down mercilessly, but they pressed on, driven by the will to survive.

The relentless journey had taken its toll on everyone, especially the younger ones. The heat and exhaustion were more than their small bodies could bear. As they trudged through the unforgiving desert, their steps grew slower, and their strength waned. Finally, with a heartbreaking collapse, the younger ones fell into the red sand, unable to go any farther.

Jax and Elara rushed to their side, panic and urgency evident in their movements. Arin and the others gathered around, their faces etched with concern and desperation. They knew they had to act quickly, as every moment in the scorching sun drained more life from their companions.

"We need to find shade and water," Jax said, his voice steady but filled with a sense of urgency. "We can't let them stay out here in the open."

Elara nodded, her eyes scanning the horizon for any sign of shelter. "We'll carry them if we have to," she said, her determination unwavering. "We have to keep moving."

The group worked together, lifting the younger ones and taking turns carrying them. Every step was a struggle, but their bonds and unwavering resolve fueled their perseverance. They knew they couldn't give up, not when the lives of their friends depended on it.

The harsh reality of their situation bore down on them as they huddled together to shield the two younger ones from the relentless sun. Jax pulled out the last piece of cloth they had to cover the girls, offering what little comfort he could. Elara's tears flowed freely as the weight of their predicament hit her. She clung to Jax and Arin, their shared despair palpable as they gazed out over the vast, unforgiving landscape.

Amidst their grief and exhaustion, they failed to notice the subtle movement beneath the red sand. It wasn't until they glanced back at the spot where the two girls had been lying that they realized the unthinkable—they were gone. The red sand had swallowed them whole without a sound, leaving no trace of their presence.

The shock and horror of the moment froze them in place. Jax's mind raced, trying to comprehend what had just happened. The sand, once a passive enemy, had now become a predator, claiming the lives of the youngest members of their group.

Desperation and sorrow weighed heavily on them, yet they knew they had to keep moving. The loss of the girls was a devastating blow, but they couldn't afford to stop now. The need to survive and honor their memory gave them a renewed sense of urgency.

The red desert had proven to be more treacherous than they could have ever imagined, but Jax, Elara, Arin, steeled themselves to face whatever lay ahead. Their journey had taken a tragic turn, but they would continue on, driven by the hope of finding a way out and the resilience that had brought them this far.

The loss of the young sisters weighed heavily on the group as they pressed forward through the relentless red desert. Their hearts ached with sorrow, each step a reminder of the tragedy they had endured. The oppressive heat and endless expanse of sand sapped their strength, but they carried on, driven by a fragile hope.

Elara, overcome with grief and exhaustion, stumbled and collapsed onto the sand. Jax and Arin, walking just ahead, turned to see her crumpled form. Before they could react, the unforgiving red sand claimed her too, silently pulling her beneath the surface. The sight left Jax and Arin in stunned disbelief, the cruel reality of their situation sinking in even deeper.

The wind howled around them, the only sound in the desolate

landscape. The desert seemed intent on erasing their very existence, one by one. Jax and Arin felt the weight of their losses, each disappearance a haunting reminder of the dangers that lurked beneath the sand.

Despite the overwhelming despair, they knew they had to keep moving. Stopping meant certain death. With heavy hearts and weary bodies, Jax and Arin continued their march through the red desert, determined to honor the memories of their fallen friends by surviving.

As they trudged onward, the vast, empty expanse offered little solace. The relentless sun beat down, draining their energy and testing their resolve. They had no choice but to rely on each other and the faint glimmers of hope that still flickered within their hearts.

The harsh reality of their situation had left Jax and Arin as the last two standing against the unforgiving red sands. With time slipping away and no way to reverse the tide, their journey had become a battle against the relentless desert and their own despair.

Their steps were heavy with sorrow and exhaustion, yet they pushed on, knowing that turning back was not an option. The memories of their lost companions fueled their determination, urging them to find a way forward despite the overwhelming odds.

The red sands stretched endlessly before them, each grain a silent reminder of the time that had slipped through their fingers. The scorching sun and the brutal environment tested their limits, but the bond between them provided a sliver of hope.

Jax and Arin, though weary and battered, were united in their resolve. They knew that their journey was not just about survival, but about honoring the memories of those they had lost. Each step forward was a testament to their strength and the unbreakable spirit that had carried them this far.

As Jax and Arin continued their desperate trek through the relentless red sands, the harsh reality of their situation became inescapable. The unforgiving desert, with its endless expanse and merciless sun, seemed to conspire against them. The memories of their lost companions weighed heavily on their hearts, pushing them forward even as their bodies faltered.

With each step, the sand seemed to grow deeper, the air hotter. Exhaustion sapped their strength until, finally, they could go no further. One by one, they too were claimed by the red sands, sinking silently beneath the surface. The relentless desert had taken its toll, and time, which once seemed infinite, had finally run out.

The vast, empty expanse of the red desert was left in eerie silence. Only the wind remained, whispering its mournful song as it swept across the dunes, a haunting reminder of the journey and the lives that had been lost. The story of Jax, Arin, and their companions had come to a poignant and somber end, echoing through the endless sands of time.

For the creature, it was left to wander the darkened rails of the abandoned subways. In the depths of the underground tunnels, where the flickering lights cast eerie shadows, it moved silently, a spectral presence in a forsaken world. The creature's fate was sealed in solitude, forever searching for a way back to the surface, to the life it once knew.

As the remnants of the past lingered in the desert and the creature roamed the forgotten subways, the echoes of their stories remained, a testament to the trials and sacrifices they endured. The journey had left indelible marks on the landscape and on the hearts of those who bore witness to their struggle. In the quiet moments, when the wind howled through the desert or threw a distant train whistle echoed in the tunnels, the memories of Jax, Arin, and their companions came alive, a whisper of their enduring legacy.

The creature, driven by a sense of loss and hope, retraced its steps through the darkened, abandoned subways. Wavering shadows that danced along the tunnel walls. Each step echoed through the deserted tunnels, a haunting reminder of its solitude.

It followed the faint scent of its companions, now lost to the relentless red sands of the desert. The scent was a comforting yet poignant reminder of their presence, urging the creature forward. As it navigated the labyrinthine passages, it hoped to find something left behind—an artifact, a piece of clothing, anything that could connect it to the ones it had lost.

The creature's journey through the tunnels was slow and deliberate. Every turn and every corner brought memories of the moments they had shared, the challenges they had faced together. It remembered their laughter, their struggles, and the bond they had formed in their quest.

Finally, in a dimly lit alcove, it found a small, weathered notebook. The creature carefully picked it up with its clawed hands, recognizing the handwriting as Arin's. Flipping through the pages, it saw sketches, notes, and thoughts that Arin had jotted down during their adventure. Tears welled up in the creature's eyes as it held the precious relic close, feeling an overwhelming sense of connection and loss.

With the notebook as its guide, the creature continued its journey, determined to honor the memory of its companions. The tunnels, once a symbol of its isolation, now held a glimmer of hope and purpose. The creature vowed to find a way back to the surface and keep the legacy of Jax, Arin, and the others alive.

The creature followed the scent back to the statue, a landmark it remembered from its journey with Jax and Arin. Its determination drove it forward, fighting through the narrow hole in the roof of the tunnel to reach the interior of the statue. The effort left it exhausted, but it was fueled by the hope of finding a piece of its lost companions' legacy.

As it finally managed to squeeze through and get inside, it collapsed onto the dusty cement floor, its chest heaving with exertion. The silence of the statue enveloped it, a stark contrast to the chaos and noise of the outside world. Lying there, it allowed itself a moment of rest, regaining its strength and reflecting on the memories of those it had lost.

The statue's interior, once a place of significance and reverence, was now a silent sanctuary for the weary creature. Dust motes floated in the shafts of light that pierced through the cracks in the walls, casting an ethereal glow over the space. The creature could feel the presence of its companions, as if their spirits lingered in this sacred place.

With renewed resolve, it began to explore its surroundings, hoping to find more remnants of Jax and Arin's journey. Every corner of the statue held potential secrets, and the creature was determined to uncover them all. As it moved through the shadows, it felt a connection to the past, a bond that transcended time and space.

The creature followed the old, broken down stairway as far as it could, each step more treacherous than the last. The structure groaned under its weight, and the disrepair made progress slow and cautious. Eventually, it reached a point where the path ahead was completely blocked, the stairs crumbling into impassable debris.

Yet, from its vantage point, it could see light streaming in from far above, a beacon of hope piercing the darkness. The light was coming in through the statue's torch-bearing hand, high above the desolate scene. The creature paused, its gaze fixed on that distant glow, feeling a renewed sense of purpose.

Determined to reach the light, it began to look for another way up. The broken stairway might have ended its direct path, but it was not the end of its journey. The creature scanned the surroundings, searching for any means to ascend further. It noticed a series of old, rusted maintenance ladders along the interior walls, leading upwards towards the light.

Carefully, it made its way to the nearest ladder, testing its stability before starting the climb. The rungs creaked and groaned under its weight, but the creature pressed on, driven by the need to reach that beacon of light. Each rung brought it closer to the torch, closer to the promise of understanding and connection.

As the creature climbed higher, the light grew brighter, illuminating its path and casting shadows that danced across the statue's interior. Finally, after a challenging ascent, it reached the platform beneath the torch. The light was almost blinding after the darkness of the tunnels, but it filled the creature with a sense of hope and clarity.

Resting for a moment, the creature looked out through the torch, seeing the vast expanse of the desert beyond. The journey had been arduous, but the creature felt a renewed determination to honor its lost companions and carry on their legacy.

It saw the twisted metal, weathered by years of relentless wind and sand, standing as a testament to time's passage. With its formidable strength, the creature approached the weakened structure. The torch, once a beacon, now crumpled under the pressure, creating an opening wide enough for the creature to squeeze through.

Inside the hollow of the statue's torch, it found a space where its companions had once hidden. The faint scent of Jax and Arin lingered in the air, barely perceptible but unmistakably familiar. Despite the fading aroma, the presence of their essence brought a sense of calm and solace to the creature. It was a connection to the past, a reminder of the bonds forged in their shared journey.

The creature stood upright, taking in the surroundings. The torch's interior was a sanctuary, a place where echoes of the past seemed to resonate. As it rested, the creature felt a deep sense of peace wash over it. Here, amidst the remnants of its companions' presence, it found the strength to continue its journey.

With renewed resolve, the creature vowed to honor the memory of Jax and Arin. Their legacy would live on, not only in the sands of the desert but also in the heart of the creature that had shared in their adventure. The journey was far from over, and the creature knew that it carried with it the spirit and determination of its lost companions.

It relaxed, allowing itself to gather strength for the journey ahead. The scent of its companions had faded, but their memory and the mission they had started drove it forward. After a moment of rest, it stood up, determined to retrace their steps and find the answers that lay beyond the confines of the subways, the creature was resolved to uncover the secrets that still lay hidden in the vast, unforgiving desert.

Breaking through to the torch, the creature was greeted by the harsh, bright light of the sun and the vast expanse of the red desert. The winds whispered their mournful song as they swept across the dunes, a stark reminder of the journey and the lives that had been lost. But the creature was undeterred. It knew that somewhere in this endless sea of sand, the answers it sought were waiting to be found.

With each step, it followed the faint traces left behind by Jax and Arin, piecing together the remnants of their travels. The journey was arduous and filled with challenges, but the creature pressed on, driven by the hope that it would honor its companions' legacy by finding the truth. The red desert was vast, but the creature's resolve was unwavering.

The creature found the carcass of the camels, a haunting reminder of the harsh reality they had faced. Scattered around were more belongings of its companions—Jax's worn-out journal, Arin's map marked with their planned route, and other personal items that carried their scent. It sniffed everything, trying to keep its mind focused and stave off the despair threatening to overwhelm it. Each familiar scent and object grounded the creature, filling it with a renewed sense of purpose.

With the relentless sun beating down on its massive body, the heat was unbearable. Every step seemed to sap more of its strength, but the creature was determined to push onward. It couldn't let the journey end here, in this desolate spot marked by loss and sorrow.

The desert stretched endlessly before it, each dune a potential landmark, each shadow a hint of the past. Despite its weakening state, the creature's resolve did not waver. It knew that the answers it sought were out there, hidden among the red sands and the distant horizon.

Driven by the memory of its companions and the hope of

uncovering the truth, the creature continued its arduous trek. The journey was far from over, and the answers were still waiting to be discovered.

The creature made its way to the old mud huts that were dug into the side of the dunes. The sight of these ancient shelters brought a sense of familiarity and solace. Weary from its arduous journey through the relentless desert, it entered the first hut it found, its eyes adjusting to the dim light filtering through the cracks.

Inside, the hut was a relic of a bygone era. Dry hay covered the floor, and broken furniture lay scattered about, telling silent tales of the lives that once filled this place. The creature carefully navigated the space, its movements slow and deliberate. It finally found a corner that offered a semblance of safety and comfort.

As it settled down on the dusty floor, the creature felt a profound sense of peace wash over it. The journey had been long and filled with hardships, but it had found a place to rest. Here, amidst the remnants of a forgotten past, it could finally lay its burdens down.

The creature closed its eyes, the memories of Jax, Arin, and their adventures still vivid in its mind. It had honored their legacy by retracing their steps and discovering the secrets they had left behind. Now, it could rest, knowing that their story would live on in the sands of time.

Without water and food, the creature sensed the end approaching. It closed its eyes, allowing sleep to gently take over. In its deep slumber, it passed away. But in those final moments, it dreamt of its new companions and the brief time they had shared. It remembered the young ones holding on to its massive back, their laughter echoing joyfully in its mind.

As it drifted deeper into sleep, these cherished memories brought a sense of peace. The bonds formed during their journey, however short-lived, provided comfort. In its dreams, the creature found solace in the companionship and the shared adventures, a testament to the resilience of friendship and the impact they had on each other's lives.

The legacy of Jax, Arin, and their companions lived on in the red sands of the desert and within the creature's final dreams. Their story, filled with determination and hope, left an indelible mark on the world.

ALSO BY KENNETH HAINES

A TALE OF ESCAPE

A group of Earthlings, including a young woman named Elara, is abducted by an invisible alien ship to become part of a cosmic exhibition. Facing the reality of being observed by an alien audience, they form a bond and ignite a longing for freedom. Together, they plot their escape, daring to dream of returning to their lives on Earth. As they navigate their captivity and fight for autonomy, they are tested but remain unbroken, driven by the hope of weaving their experiences back into humanity's story.

WHISPERS IN THE SAND

Amidst the whispers of the sand and the caress of the Autumn sea, a tale of survival unfolds on the shores of a forsaken island. Here, young Selene and her father carve out an existence, relying on the embrace of nature and each other. Their bond, once threatened by tragedy, burgeons under the trials they face in this barren refuge. But when the island yields an unexpected reunion, the fabric of their family is woven together once more, painting a poignant portrait of hope and resilience. In the cool embrace of a late afternoon's breeze, Selene's heart finds solace, and together, they etch a new beginning upon their souls—an indelible whisper in the fabric of time.

TYLORIN

In the oppressive kingdom of Eldaf, where elves endure human cruelty, a desperate elf mother and her child find an unexpected ally in a compassionate human. Together, they embark on a perilous escape through secret paths and natural sanctuaries, aided by the whispers of the forest's denizens. Their journey leads them to an abandoned, tranquil cottage, where they begin a new life of resilience and love. United by courage and kinship, their bond transcends blood, offering hope and peace amidst the shadows of their past.

ECHOES OF LAUGHTER, ECHOES OF FEAR

In an abandoned amusement park reclaimed by nature, five young explorersâ€"three girls and two boysâ€"embark on an adventure filled with mystery and spectral intrigue. Amid peeling paint and rusting rides, they delve into the park's hidden sorrows, blending nostalgia with a sense of foreboding. As they confront both the park's secrets and their own fears, their journey becomes a test of courage, friendship, and the human spirit. In this eerie yet captivating odyssey, the line between joy and darkness blurs, leaving them to discover whether their bonds can light the way through the park's enigmatic shadows.

SEA OF SHADOWS

Stranded on a solitary island, young Helene navigates a journey of survival and self-discovery, guided by the wisdom of her late father and the lessons of the untamed wilderness. Amid the island's deceptive tranquility, she transforms grief into resilience, building a sanctuary from remnants of the past and forging a future shaped by love and fortitude. Through hardship, Helene finds strength in enduring connections, her father's presence ever a guiding light. Her odyssey is one of emotional catharsis and renewal, where each dawn heralds the triumph of hope and the radiance of new beginnings.

www.ingramcontent.com/pod-product-compliance
Lightning Source LLC
LaVergne TN
LVHW010507160826
845677LV00012B/2703

* 9 7 9 8 8 9 6 9 1 3 3 9 9 *